Railway Series, No. 1

THE
THREE RAILWAY ENGINES

First published by
Edmund Ward (Publishers) Ltd 1945
Twenty fourth impression by Kaye & Ward Ltd
The Windmill Press, Kingswood, Tadworth, Surrey
1984

ISBN 0 7182 0000 4

Printed and bound in Great Britain by
William Clowes Limited, Beccles and London

Railway Series, No. 1

THE
THREE RAILWAY ENGINES

by

THE REV. W. AWDRY

with illustrations by
C. REGINALD DALBY

KAYE & WARD LIMITED

Edward's Day Out

ONCE upon a time there was a little engine called Edward. He lived in a shed with five other engines. They were all bigger than Edward and boasted about it. "The driver won't choose you again," they said. "He wants big, strong engines like us." Edward had not been out for a long time; he began to feel sad.

Just then the driver and fireman came along to start work.

The driver looked at Edward. "Why are you sad?" he asked. "Would you like to come out today?"

"Yes, please," said Edward. So the fireman lit the fire and made a nice lot of steam.

Then the driver pulled the lever, and Edward puffed away.

"Peep, peep," he whistled. "Look at me now."

The others were very cross at being left behind.

Away went Edward to get some coaches.

"Be careful, Edward," said the coaches, "don't bump and bang us like the other engines do." So Edward came up to the coaches, very, very gently, and the shunter fastened the coupling.

"Thank you, Edward," said the coaches. "That was kind, we are glad you are taking us today."

Then they went to the station where the people were waiting.

"Peep, peep," whistled Edward—"get in quickly, please."

So the people got in quickly and Edward waited happily for the guard to blow his whistle, and wave his green flag.

He waited and waited—there was no whistle, no green flag. "Peep, peep, peep, peep—where is that guard?" Edward was getting anxious.

The driver and fireman asked the Stationmaster, "Have you seen the guard?" "No," he said. They asked the porter, "Have you seen the guard?" "Yes—last night," said the porter.

Edward began to get cross. "Are we ever going to start?" he said.

Just then a little boy shouted, "Here he comes!" and there the guard was, running down the hill with his flags in one hand and a sandwich in the other.

He ran on to the platform, blew his whistle, and jumped into his van.

Edward puffed off. He did have a happy day. All the children ran to wave as he went past and he met old friends at all the stations. He worked so hard that the driver promised to take him out again next day.

"I'm going out again tomorrow," he told the other engines that night in the shed. "What do you think of that?"

But he didn't hear what they thought, for he was so tired and happy that he fell asleep at once.

Edward and Gordon

ONE of the engines in Edward's shed was called Gordon. He was very big and very proud.

"You watch me this afternoon, little Edward," he boasted, "as I rush through with the express; that will be a splendid sight for you."

Just then his driver pulled the lever. "Goodbye, little Edward," said Gordon, as he puffed away, "look out for me this afternoon!"

Edward went off, too, to do some shunting.

Edward liked shunting. It was fun playing with trucks. He would come up quietly and give them a pull.

"Oh! Oh! Oh! Oh! Oh!" screamed the trucks. "Whatever is happening?"

Then he would stop and the silly trucks would go bump into each other. "Oh! Oh! Oh! Oh!" they cried again.

Edward pushed them until they were running nicely, and when they weren't expecting it he would stop; one of them would be sure to run on to another line. Edward played till

there were no more trucks; then he stopped to rest.

Presently he heard a whistle. Gordon came puffing along, very slowly, and very crossly. Instead of nice shining coaches, he was pulling a lot of very dirty coal trucks.

"A goods train! a goods train! a goods train!" he grumbled. "The shame of it, the shame of it, the shame of it."

He went slowly through, with the trucks clattering and banging behind him.

Edward laughed, and went to find some more trucks.

Soon afterwards a porter came and spoke to his driver. "Gordon can't get up the hill. Will you take Edward and push him, please?"

They found Gordon halfway up the hill and very cross. His driver and fireman were talking to him severely. "You are not trying!" they told him.

"I can't do it," said Gordon. "The noisy trucks hold an engine back so. If they were coaches now—clean sensible things that come quietly—that would be different."

Edward's driver came up. "We've come to push," he said. "No use at all," said Gordon. "You wait and see," said Edward's driver.

They brought the train back to the bottom of the hill. Edward came up behind the brake van ready to push.

"Peep, peep, I'm ready," said Edward.

"Poop, poop, no good," grumbled Gordon.

The guard blew his whistle and they pulled and pushed as hard as they could.

"I can't do it, I can't do it, I can't do it," puffed Gordon.

"I will do it, I will do it, I will do it," puffed Edward.

"I can't do it, I will do it, I can't do it, I will do it, I can't do it, I will do it," they puffed together.

Edward pushed and puffed and puffed and pushed, as hard as ever he could, and almost before he realized it, Gordon found himself at the top of the hill.

"I've done it! I've done it! I've done it!" he said proudly, and forgot all about Edward pushing behind. He didn't wait to say "Thank you", but ran on so fast that he passed two stations before his driver could make him stop.

Edward had pushed so hard that when he got to the top he was out of breath.

Gordon ran on so fast that Edward was left behind.

The guard waved and waved, but Edward couldn't catch up.

He ran on to the next station, and there the driver and fireman said they were very pleased with him. The fireman gave him a nice long drink of water, and the driver said, "I'll get out my paint tomorrow, and give you a beautiful new coat of blue with red stripes, then you'll be the smartest engine in the shed."

The Sad Story of Henry

ONCE, an engine attached to a train

Was afraid of a few drops of rain—

—It went into a tunnel,

And squeaked through its funnel

And never came out again.

The engine's name was Henry. His driver and fireman argued with him, but he would not move. "The rain will spoil my lovely green paint and red stripes," he said.

The guard blew his whistle till he had no more breath, and waved his flags till his arms ached; but Henry still stayed in the tunnel, and blew steam at him.

"I am not going to spoil my lovely green paint and red stripes for you," he said rudely.

The passengers came and argued too, but Henry would not move.

A fat director who was on the train told the guard to get a rope. "We will pull you out," he said. But Henry only blew steam at him and made him wet.

They hooked the rope on and all pulled—except the fat director. "My doctor has forbidden me to pull," he said.

They pulled and pulled and pulled, but still Henry stayed in the tunnel.

Then they tried pushing from the other end. The fat director said, "One, two, three, push": but did not help. "My doctor has forbidden me to push," he said.

They pushed and pushed and pushed; but still Henry stayed in the tunnel.

At last another train came. The guard waved his red flag and stopped it. The two engine drivers, the two firemen, and the two guards

went and argued with Henry. "Look, it has stopped raining," they said. "Yes, but it will begin again soon," said Henry. "And what would become of my green paint with red stripes then?"

So they brought the other engine up, and it pushed and puffed, and puffed and pushed as hard as ever it could. But still Henry stayed in the tunnel.

So they gave it up. They told Henry, "We shall leave you there for always and always and always."

They took up the old rails, built a wall in front of him, and cut a new tunnel.

Now Henry can't get out, and he watches the trains rushing through the new tunnel. He is very sad because no one will ever see his lovely green paint with red stripes again.

But I think he deserved it, don't you?

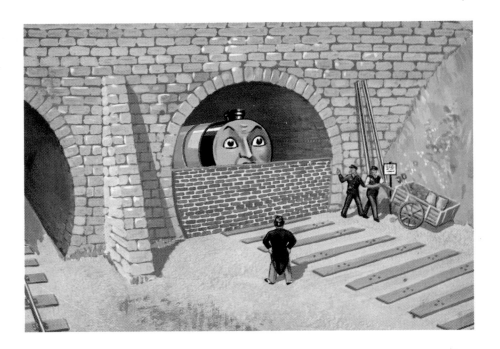

Edward, Gordon and Henry

EDWARD and Gordon often went through the tunnel where Henry was shut up.

Edward would say, "Peep, peep—hullo!" and Gordon would say, "Poop, poop, poop! Serves you right!"

Poor Henry had no steam to answer, his fire had gone out; soot and dirt from the tunnel roof had spoilt his lovely green paint and red stripes. He was cold and unhappy, and wanted to come out and pull trains too.

Gordon always pulled the express. He was proud of being the only engine strong enough to do it.

There were many heavy coaches, full of important people like the fat director who had punished Henry.

Gordon was seeing how fast he could go. "Hurry! hurry! hurry!" he panted.

"Trickety-trock, trickety-trock, trickety-trock," said the coaches.

Gordon could see Henry's tunnel in front.

"In a minute," he thought, "I'll poop, poop, poop at Henry, and rush through and out into the open again."

Closer and closer he came—he was almost there, when crack: "Wheee ———————— eeshshsh," he was in a cloud of steam, and going slower and slower.

His driver stopped the train.

"What has happened to me?" asked Gordon, "I feel so weak." "You've burst your safety valve," said the driver. "You can't pull the train any more." "Oh, dear," said Gordon. "We were going so nicely, too. .... Look at Henry laughing at me." Gordon made a face at Henry, and blew smoke at him.

Everybody got out, and came to see Gordon. "Humph!" said the fat director. "I never liked these big engines—always going wrong; send for another engine at once."

While the guard went to find one, they uncoupled Gordon, and ran him on a siding out of the way.

The only engine left in the shed was Edward.

"I'll come and try," he said.

Gordon saw him coming. "That's no use," he said, "Edward can't pull the train."

Edward puffed and pulled, and pulled and puffed, but he couldn't move the heavy coaches.

"I told you so," said Gordon rudely. "Why not let Henry try?"

"Yes," said the fat director, "I will."

"Will you help pull this train, Henry?" he asked. "Yes," said Henry at once.

So Gordon's driver and fireman lit his fire; some platelayers broke down the wall and put back the rails; and when he had steam up Henry puffed out.

He was dirty, his boiler was black, and he was covered with cobwebs. "Ooh! I'm so stiff! Ooh! I'm so stiff!" he groaned.

"You'd better have a run to ease your joints, and find a turntable," said the fat director kindly.

Henry came back feeling better, and they put him in front.

"Peep, peep," said Edward, "I'm ready."

"Peep, peep, peep," said Henry, "so am I."

"Pull hard; pull hard; pull hard," puffed Edward.

"We'll do it; we'll do it; we'll do it," puffed Henry.

"Pull hard we'll do it. Pull hard we'll do it. Pull hard we'll do it," they puffed together. The heavy coaches jerked and began to move, slowly at first, then faster and faster.

"We've done it together! We've done it together! We've done it together!" said Edward and Henry.

"You've done it, hurray! You've done it, hurray! You've done it, hurray!" sang the coaches.

All the passengers were excited. The fat director leaned out of the window to wave to Edward and Henry; but the train was going so fast that his hat blew off into a field where a goat ate it for his tea.

They never stopped till they came to the big station at the end of the line.

The passengers all got out and said, "Thank you," and the fat director promised Henry a new coat of paint.

"Would you like blue and red?"

"Yes, please," said Henry, "then I'll be like Edward."

Edward and Henry went home quietly, and on their way they helped Gordon back to the shed.

All three engines are now great friends.

Wasn't Henry pleased when he had his new coat. He is very proud of it, as all good engines are—but he doesn't mind the rain now, because he knows that the best way to keep his paint nice is not to run into tunnels, but to ask his driver to rub him down when the day's work is over.

The Rev. W. Awdry Railway Series

POP-UP BOOKS

Eight titles now available with paper mechanics by Roy Laming and pictures by Clive Spong.

Thomas the Tank Engine Goes Fishing
Bertie the Bus and Thomas the Tank Engine
Henry the Green Engine Gets Out
The Flying Kipper and Henry the Green Engine
James the Red Engine and the Troublesome Trucks
Thomas the Tank Engine and the Tractor
Percy the Small Engine Takes the Plunge
Henry the Green Engine and the Elephant

MAP OF THE ISLAND OF SODOR

Sodor, situated between Barrow-in-Furness and the Isle of Man is where Thomas, Henry, James, Edward, Gordon and the other engines have their adventures. This colourful map, measuring 560 × 760 mm when open, makes an excellent wall decoration. There is a key to many of the places where incidents in the books take place.